Don't count the number of birthdays.
Count how happy you feel. I'm Birthday
Bear, and I'll help make your birthdays
the best ever.

I'm Wish Bear, and if
you wish on my star,
maybe your special dream
will come true.

If you're ever feeling lonely,
just call on me, Friend Bear.
See, I've got a daisy for you
and a daisy for me.

Grr! I'm Grumpy Bear. There's a cloud on
my tummy to show that I take the grouchies
away, so you can be happy again.

I'm Love-a-Lot Bear. I have two
hearts on my tummy. One is for you;
the other is for someone you love.

It's my job to bring you sweet dreams.
I'm Bedtime Bear, and right now I'm a bit
sleepy. Are you sleepy, too?

Now that you know all of us, we hope
that you'll have a special place for us in your
heart, just like we do for you.

With love from all of us,

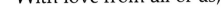

The Care Bears

Published in the United States by Parker Brothers, Division of CPG Products Corp.

Care Bears, Care Bears Logo, Tenderheart Bear, Friend Bear, Grumpy Bear, Birthday Bear, Cheer Bear, Bedtime Bear, Funshine Bear, Love-a-Lot
Bear, Wish Bear and Good Luck Bear are trademarks of American Greetings Corporation, Parker Brothers, authorized user.

Library of Congress Cataloging in Publication Data: Mason, Evelyn. A sister for Sam. SUMMARY: Cheer Bear, a Care Bear from the land of Care-a-lot who always knows the right thing to say, helps Sam overcome his anxiety and resentment against his brand new baby sister.
[1. Brothers and sisters—Fiction. 2. Sibling rivalry—Fiction. 3. Babies—Fiction. 4. Bears—Fiction] I. Cooke, Tom, ill. II. Title. PZ7.M388Si 1982 [E] 83-2236 ISBN 0-910313-03-2
Manufactured in the United States of America   7 8 9 0

A Tale from the
Care Bears

A Sister for Sam

Story by Evelyn Mason
Pictures by Tom Cooke

It was morning. Sam could tell by the noises and
the smells. He could hear water running in the shower,
and he could smell bacon cooking in the kitchen.

Sam rolled over and jumped out of bed and went
to find his father and his mother.

"Here I am, Daddy. Where's Mommy?"

Daddy picked Sam up and said, "I have something to tell you. Last night while you were asleep I took Mommy to the hospital. This morning you have a baby sister. Her name is Emily."

"Who stayed with me while you were gone?" asked Sam.

"Grandma. She's in the kitchen right now. If you go downstairs, I'm sure she'll give you your breakfast."

After Sam gave Grandma a good-morning hug, he had many questions to ask.

"How big is my sister?"

"Does she have hair?"

"What can she do?"

"Will she talk to me?"

Grandma answered, "Emily weighs a little less than your cat—about eight pounds. She can't say anything yet, but she does know how to cry."

"And when will Mommy be home?" asked Sam.

"Mommy will be home in three days. Then you'll be able to see just what Emily is like," said Grandma.

After breakfast Sam went to his room and sat on his bed. There were questions that he hadn't dared ask Grandma:

"Will I like this baby?"

"Will this baby like me?"

He wished there were someone who could answer those questions.

Three days later a fat bundle was brought home from the hospital. Everyone, including Sam, watched Mommy unwrap the baby.

"Isn't she pretty," said Grandma.

"Isn't she cute," said Aunt Ellen.

"Isn't she sweet," said Uncle George.

"Isn't she lovely," said Grandpa.

Sam wondered why everybody was making such a fuss over a sleeping baby.

Aunt Ellen gave Emily a stuffed animal. Uncle George took some pictures. Sam thought, "I don't know why everyone is so interested in Emily. She's boring. She doesn't even talk."

Then Sam went to his room.

It was raining and Sam stared out the window. He
needed someone to talk to.

Suddenly a rainbow shone in the sky and, behind him, Sam heard a cheery voice saying, "I'm sure that your baby sister is going to like you. And most of the time you are going to like her, too."

Sam turned around and there, sitting in his chair, was a smiling bear with a rainbow shining on its tummy.

"Who are you? And where do you come from?"
Sam asked.

"My name is Cheer Bear. Let's just say rainbows
and I sometimes come together. I think I can help
answer your questions. I'll stay around a while if that's
all right with you."

Sam thought that sounded like a
good idea, for he did have things
to say.

"Cheer Bear," he said, "I don't think I like my new baby sister."

Cheer Bear, who always knew just the right thing to say, answered, "Sometimes you may feel left out when your sister gets a lot of attention. You may even say to yourself, 'Mommy and Daddy don't love me anymore; they just love Emily.' They do love you, you know, but when you feel that way, be sure to come and tell me. I'll give you a warm bear hug."

Emily cried a lot at first. Sometimes it seemed that she cried day and night.

When Emily's crying woke him up, Sam turned to Cheer Bear and said, "Why can't Emily *say* something, instead of making all that noise!"

Cheer Bear, who always knew just the right thing to say, answered, "Sometimes Emily is a bother to all of us. I know that you don't like it when Emily cries. When you feel that way, talk to me. If you tell me, you won't feel so angry inside."

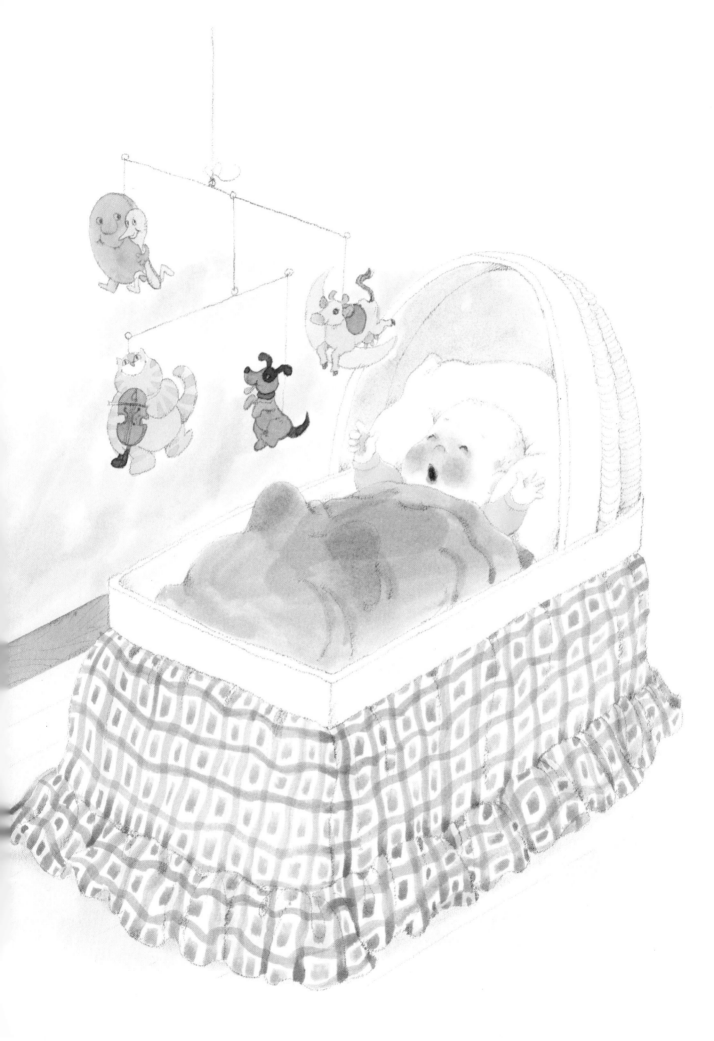

When Emily wasn't crying, she was usually sleeping. And whenever she woke up, her diaper needed changing. Then she needed milk and sometimes another diaper.

Sam had to wait for what he needed. And he didn't like that one bit.

Sometimes Sam pretended that Emily wasn't there.

Sometimes he tried to interrupt.

Sometimes he stamped his feet and shouted.

When that happened, Sam was usually sent to his room.

Sam would lie on his bed and not talk to anybody—or he would hide under the bed.

When Sam felt a little better, he would talk to Cheer Bear. "Bear, he said, "sometimes Emily makes me so mad."

Cheer Bear, who always knew just the right thing to say, answered, "Sam, I know that you are angry. Show me how angry you are, and I'll watch."

And Cheer Bear watched Sam throw his toys on the floor and cry. When Sam finished crying, he and Cheer Bear played a game.

"You know, Sam," said Cheer Bear, "Emily won't always be so small. She is going to grow and become more interesting."

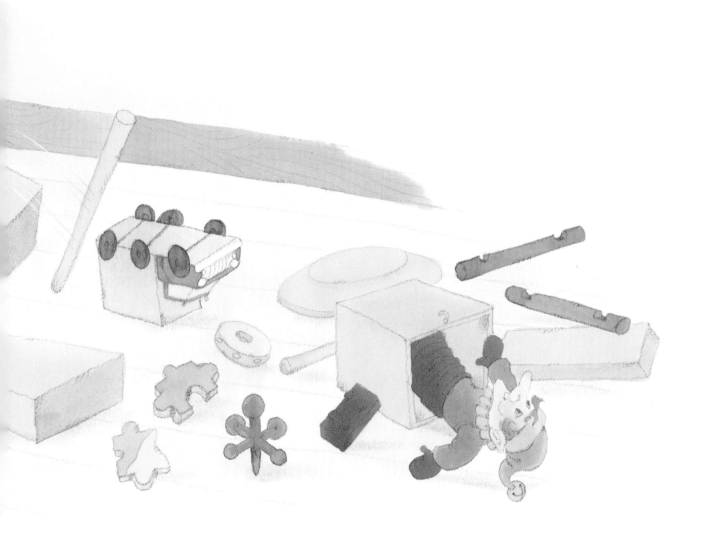

Emily did grow, and she did become more interesting, just as Cheer Bear said she would.

Emily learned to roll over

to smile

to hold things

and to make noises.

Emily learned to sit up

then to crawl

and finally to stand.
   The hair on her head
turned to curls and
the smile on her
face turned to
giggles.

Mommy and Daddy said, "I know Emily likes you a lot."

"How do they know?" Sam thought. "Emily doesn't talk."

Now that Emily could move around she got into Sam's things.

Emily could knock down a building

tear a picture

pull a book from the shelf
and throw a truck on the floor.

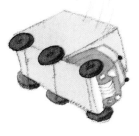

Whenever Emily made a mess, Sam got mad.
Sometimes Sam got so mad, he would try to make
Emily cry.

Sam soon found out that scaring Emily did not make her cry. Emily just made noises: "Noonoo . . . bahbah . . . goo!"

And those noises made Sam even madder.

Sam told Cheer Bear
what he thought.
"Bear," he asked, "when
will those silly noises stop?
I want to talk to Emily."
Cheer Bear, who always
knew just the right thing to
say, answered, "I think
Emily is getting ready to
talk. Making noises is her
way of practicing."

Sam decided to help Emily learn to talk.
"Ball—say ball."
"Goo!" said Emily.
"Truck—say truck."
"Ga!" said Emily.

"Cat—say cat."
"Goo-ga!" said Emily.

Every day Sam tried to teach Emily a word. And every day Emily made different noises.

Emily even made noises at Bear.

"Bear—say bear." But Emily only grinned.

At Emily's first birthday party, everyone wondered what her first word would be.

"I'm sure that it will be *Mama*," said Sam's mother.

"I'm sure it will be *Daddy*," said Sam's father.

"I'm sure it will be *Sam*," said Sam.

In the middle of the party Mother said, "Shh! I think Emily is talking. She is trying to say something."

Everyone listened. Emily did not say *Mama*. Emily did not say *Daddy*. Emily did not say *Sam*. Emily said, "Bear!"

Sam was happy. Emily had said a word that was special to him. Emily was going to be an okay sister.

Then Sam looked up and smiled. For there, outside in the sky, was a rainbow.